Mili & Gaja Go on a Posting

Anisha Kotibhaskar
Co-Author Dr. Sunanda Roy

Ukiyoto Publishing

All global publishing rights are held by

Ukiyoto Publishing

Published in 2024

Content Copyright © Anisha Kotibhaskar
Co-Author Dr. Sunanda Roy

ISBN 9789367958278

*All rights reserved.
No part of this publication may be reproduced,
transmitted, or stored in a retrieval system, in any
form by any means, electronic, mechanical,
photocopying, recording or otherwise, without the
prior permission of the publisher.*

The moral rights of the authors have been asserted.

*This is a work of fiction. Names, characters, businesses,
places, events, locales, and incidents are either the
products of the author's imagination or used in a
fictitious manner. Any resemblance to actual persons,
living or dead, or actual events is purely coincidental.*

*This book is sold subject to the condition that it shall
not by way of trade or otherwise, be lent, resold, hired
out or otherwise circulated, without the publisher's
prior consent, in any form of binding or cover other
than that in which it is published.*

www.ukiyoto.com

For my dearest Ahana.

Contents

Chapter 1: The Train Compartment	1
Chapter 2: The Girl with the Mismatched Socks	7
Chapter 3: The Post-Ink	12
Chapter 4: A Fan Inside a Trunk and a Mind Map!	17
Chapter 5: The Final Goodbye	23
Chapter 6: An Elephant on the Belt	28
Chapter 7: A Shared New House	33
Chapter 8: A Sweet Treat, But for Whom?	39
Chapter 9: A New Neighbour	45
Chapter 10: The Housewarming Party	51
Play with Mili!	61
About the Authors	66

Chapter 1: The Train Compartment

There was no one in the house. Everything was quiet. Some birds were chirping outside, and even though it was late afternoon, the bright sun was making everything look yellow. In the hot month of July, this quiet town of Alagpur in the northern parts of India was making everyone go nuts.

Click, clunk, chuck.

"…hee hee hee."

"Krdm, krdum…"

There was someone in the house, and they were eating something crunchy!

The sound of the giggle was unmistakable. In one of the rooms, Mili and her friend Kiva were travelling to a far-off place in their secret train compartment, which happened to be inside a cupboard. The open side of the space was covered with a curtain, and it was their window. As they looked outside the window, they saw running trees, stomping dinosaurs, and chocolate-laden houses. They were munching on some bhakarwadis that Mili's ajji (grandmother) had sent from Thane.

"Run Kiva. Run! The dinosaur is coming after us."

"Where can we run? We are already on a train. Don't worry, in a minute, we will reach my castle."

"It's mine too! I built it with jelly toffies!"

"Then, let's be careful at night. We don't want ants attacking us."

"Stop imagining ants on you. It's just a pretend game!"

"It's not. This train is real, our castle is real…"

Mili and Kiva were nothing like each other. When Mili laughed loudly, Kiva would chuckle. If Mili loved to crack a joke aloud, Kiva loved to make herself invisible to Mili and secretly smile in hiding. Mili had the twist-iest curls and Kiva had the straightest of hairs. Mili was a Maharashtrian, and all Mili knew was that Kiva wasn't. That's what made them best friends that summer.

But on this train, they were not the sole travellers. There was a doll, a dog, a pig, a turtle and Gaja. They were all travelling peacefully to their destination until Kiva took charge of the pig, Pebbles.

"Come let me give you some food. You must be hungry!"

"Pebbles is my baby," claimed Mili.

"No, I like him too. He is mine," asserted Kiva.

"But he was gifted to me by my papa!" shouted Mili.

"But his straight hair matches mine!" squeaked Kiva.

"So what? Your hair is straight, and your mama's hair is not! It's not necessary to have the same type of hair," squeaked Mili.

"But you have Gaja!" Kiva squeaked louder.

"The last time you fought over that funny-looking pig, he was locked up in the trunk for a month. I'm just saying," Gaja reminded Mili.

Finally, the squeaking was over.

Gaja was a greyish-blue elephant with just one eye on him, and yet he could see everything going on around him. Gaja was Mili's real baby, or at least that's what she believed.

Mili paused. Gaja was right, but it wasn't easy to give up. Mili gave a quick thought and came up with a plan. "Ok, take him till we reach the next station, and then…"

Mili & Gaja Go on a Posting

Mili's plan was cut short with her mother walking in. Mili had forgotten that Mama was at home too! She was quietly working all this while, like most grown-ups do. How do they manage? Anyway, everyone called her Radha.

"Not again, girls. There are some puzzles, blocks, and balls for playing too. Why don't you both try those?"

"Not now!" Mili replied, and Kiva joined in. Soon they were busy setting up their compartment for the next journey. Pebbles was forgotten. Radha's presence was forgotten.

Radha murmured, "I must take them to the park tomorrow," and went back to checking the notebooks of the children in her class, only to get up again in the next seven seconds.

Crash!

"I don't know how one can drop so many things in a day!" thought Radha. She pushed aside her chair to get up and accidentally spilt a glass of water. Thankfully they just missed the notebooks. She quickly looked around to check if anyone saw her.

Nikhil walked in and said, "Sorry, I spilt *dahi* (curd) kept in the fridge. In my defence, it was terribly arranged, precariously kept on top of two more containers!"

"Major Nikhil Joshi, I told you, we need a new fridge!"

Mili, holding Gaja by his trunk, and Kiva walked to see what the chaos was about. Mili saw her father had just returned from the office because he was still wearing his olive-green uniform. He was an army officer, he protected the country, or so she heard. 'Protecting the country' was his job. What did he really protect the country from?

Chapter 2: The Girl with the Mismatched Socks

Mili, Kiva, and Radha walked into the park the next evening. Mili was holding Gaja by his trunk. The sun followed them everywhere, and everything still looked yellow. Drops of sweat were dripping down their foreheads, and everyone else's. But only the grown-ups were seen to be wiping them off. Lots of children were playing on the swings.

The young ones pestered their mothers to take them higher. The 8–10-year-olds were going so high that it seemed they would circle back. The trio's walk from the gate to the slides was back and forth, as Mili kept stopping to pick up interesting stones and seeds fallen from the trees.

On their way to the slides, Mili and Kiva noticed two girls sitting on the ground and up to something. Mili and Kiva couldn't hear them; maybe they were too far away.

"What do you think they are playing?" asked Mili.

Kiva shrugged. So, it meant they had to go and see.

As they approached the two girls, they still couldn't hear anything. The girls were busy making something.

"What are you making?" asked Mili.

"A nest," answered the girl who seemed to be wearing mismatched socks – a yellow one with stripes and another yellow one with polka dots. The other who didn't have mismatched socks, rather who wasn't wearing any socks, picked a stick and showed five of her fingers to her friend. Off went the friend to get something. There were already seven nests made. Mili and Kiva observed them carefully, amused with the neat and beautiful nest.

"Can we also make one?" asked Mili. The no-socks girl grinned and nodded.

The mismatched-socks girl was back by then with five sticks, making the other one happy. Mili watched the no-socks girl do something with her hands again. Off went her friend again, to pluck some berries from the nearby bush.

Now, the no-socks girl looked at Mili and Kiva. She pointed at an empty spot and made some hand gestures looking at the spot and then looking at Mili and Kiva.

After a few seconds of silence, lots of gestures, and utter confusion, Mili and Kiva burst out laughing. No-socks girl burst into tears and ran to her friend.

Mili watched her mother walk to the girl and comfort her. A few minutes later, Radha was back.

"I didn't do anything," squeaked Mili.

"It's fine, Mili," replied Radha, not wanting to spend even an ounce of energy. Humidity was killing.

After a while, sensing that things were okay, Mili asked Radha on the way home, "Why wasn't the girl talking? I really couldn't understand what she was saying."

"Because, Millilitre, she can't talk," replied her mother.

"Why, she is taller and bigger than me and I can talk," replied Mili, almost feeling like a big girl.

"Sometimes, some people can't."

"Can she walk and jump?" asked Mili.

"Of course!"

"Can she write?" joined in Kiva.

"Of course."

"Does she go to school?" asked Mili.

"Yes, of course."

"Can she hear?" asked Kiva.

"Yes, in fact much better than you!"

"Can we be her friends?" asked Mili, and Kiva joined in, "Will she be friends with us?"

"There can be nothing better than that. Now, let's go home," replied the mother.

As they were walking out of the park, Gaja couldn't hold it in. He raised his only eye and asked Mili, "I have one eye, and I am your best friend, am I not?"

Chapter 3: The Post-Ink

After dinner, Mili had just tucked Gaja in a bed made of a shoebox, with her little towels as Gaja's blankets when she heard her Mama and Papa discuss something while clearing up the kitchen and the dining table.

The voices sounded different, which meant they were definitely discussing something really, really important. She went in, holding the reluctant Gaja by his trunk. Mili's Papa was still in his uniform, having just come back from the office.

Mama and Papa exchanged looks. Finally, Radha nodded and kneeled before Mili.

This was going to be serious. Mili kept Gaja aside.

"Well, something has come up Mili. We just got the news of your papa's posting. Looks like we will now be moving to a new place."

"Like a holiday?"

"No, not a holiday. It's called a posting."

"Will there be snow or a beach at this... post-ink?"

"None. All of us will be shifting with all our things. We'll be getting another house to stay in."

"All of us?"

"Of course!"

"When do we start packing?"

"Let's see. We will plan it out and then start," replied Nikhil.

"How will we pack the bed?"

"Millilitre," said Radha in a calm voice. Mili wondered why Radha was calling her Millilitre, the name she used when she wanted to be extra cautious and patient. "It's not ours. We will leave it here for the next person to take it over. We will be given another one once we reach the next place."

"Oh! And has Kiva also started packing? I will ask her tomorrow."

Radha and Nikhil burst out laughing.

Mili wasn't pleased. "Don't laugh!" said Mili firmly, blowing the noodle hair off her forehead.

"Sorry... Millilitre. But nobody is coming with us. It's just the three of us."

Mili felt her lips curling, and tears building up in her eyes. "But you said, all of us..." Mili looked at her mother as if she had taken away her greatest joy.

"I meant, ALL three of us. I am sorry if you understood otherwise."

"I don't want to go."

"But we have to."

"OK, after a few days can we come back here?"

"I don't think that will be possible."

"But Kiva will miss me!"

Mili grabbed Gaja who was silently listening and went into her train compartment.

Once settled, Gaja asked, "Would you call that 'a bad behaviour'?"

"I don't know...why?"

"Well, usually one gets the dessert only if one has been good. And there is some kulfi in the fridge. Yesterday there were seven, and then three of you ate one each. Then, papa ate one more, and then one more, as usual. So, that makes it two in the freezer at this moment. How do you feel about that? I've heard adults can absent-mindedly do things when in a discussion."

Mili's eyes lit up and she sprinted to the dining room.

"OK, I will come with you for the post-ink." After a pause, she added eyeing the freezer, "Is there anything for dessert?"

Chapter 4: A Fan Inside a Trunk and a Mind Map!

A few days went by. Trunks were lined up everywhere. They were big, painted black, with Maj Nikhil Joshi and a serial number written on them.

All Mili heard in those days and later were words like trunks, posting, packing, bubble wrap, and truck.

It was Sunday. Mili wanted to be a part of the excitement. She got on with packing her stuff. With great conviction, she grabbed her honeybee backpack. One by one, she chose her priciest possessions — some of her favourite seeds from her collection, ten imli (tamarind) toffees, seven bangles, five jam biscuits, two storybooks, one t-shirt, one pair of pants, one frock, one undergarment, one water bottle, one set of crayons, one drawing book, one toy car, one wooden doll, and in the end, the one-and-only, Gaja.

The bag was stuffed, and it now resembled a ball. Poor Gaja's trunk was folded in a spiral. His trunk was squeezed into a ball and his only eye was peeping out through the small opening where the zip wouldn't close.

"I can't breathe!"

"Oh sorry, then you be in my hand. Now, let's go."

Nikhil had just arrived from the office at noon, and Mili had just finished packing.

She walked in when Radha and Nikhil were setting up the table for lunch.

"I have finished my packing," Mili beamed.

The parents hid their amused smiles.

"That's great Mili. But we still have a month to go. Anyway, now you can help us pack other things from tomorrow."

The first thing Mili said the next morning when she opened her eyes was, "What are we packing today? The fan?" She looked up and wondered how it could fit in a trunk.

"I think we'll need a bigger trunk for it..."

"That's not ours, Mili. We won't be taking it," said Radha as she was getting ready for school.

"Then, the dining table?"

"That's not ours," replied Radha as she prepared the breakfast.

"The garden chairs?"

"Not ours again," replied Nikhil as he wore his uniform.

"The cabinet?"

"Nope," replied Radha as she got Mili ready for school.

"How about..."

Radha interrupted, "Millilitre, you know what, let's make a mind map."

"What's a mind map?"

"A mind map is a map of your thoughts. Something that helps you sort out your thoughts and come up with a logical plan of action."

All this sounded like something adults would do, so Mili instantly replied "Okay!"

Radha took a quick peek at her watch and sighed. It was 7 a.m., and she had just a few minutes to spare before heading to the school.

She made Mili sit down with a piece of paper.

She explained as she drew. "We first make a drawing in the centre and write the name of the thing we are planning. Like a birthday party, or a posting or packing in our case."

Radha drew a trunk in the centre circle and wrote *'Mili's Packing'* inside it.

"Now, what are the things you need to think of for packing."

"I know, a suitcase. I will put everything in a suitcase. Draw it!"

"Not like that sweetheart. First, you think of the things you need to pack.

Radha made a wavy branch starting from the circle in the centre– *Clothes*.

"What else?" she asked.

"Books?" asked Mili.

Radha made another wavy branch from the circle - *Books*

"Now, amongst books, you have schoolbooks and storybooks." Radha made two curvy lines starting from Books; one for schoolbooks, and one for storybooks.

"Toys?"

Radha made another branch - *Toys*

"Shoes?"

"Yes, and maybe all other things would go as *Miscellaneous*," Radha concluded looking at her watch.

"Miss-lay-knee-us?"

"Meaning other random things."

Together they built the sub-branches of each of the branches of the mind map and finally left for school.

Chapter 5: The Final Goodbye

Mili was busy. She was running in and out of the house through the two types of doors at each entrance. But that was just the main door. There were seven others in the house! The main door had a net door, and the other door was made of wood. The net doors were to be kept closed so that mosquitoes could stay out, while the wooden doors were to be kept open so that air could come in.

All rules were broken today because a huge truck was standing right outside, and their wooden and steel trunks were being loaded on it. The doors had to be kept open.

Inside, all the rooms were full of trunks, and the floor was scattered with Mili's seeds. As the furniture had been moved, the seeds were found lurking in every corner of the house.

"Where shall we put this?" asked Mili, picking up a worn-out bag kept aside for discarding.

But nobody heard as everyone was outside planning how to arrange the trunks in the truck. So, she kept it neatly in the shoe trunk kept in that room.

"And this?" she murmured, picking up some plastic containers kept aside for giving away. She put them in the trunk that had *razai*s (blankets) stored in them.

"And this?" she exclaimed as she found her lost (and now found) finger puppet. She looked up, and finally, there was someone who heard her.

Did he understand her, maybe not, because he was a stray dog! He was blankly staring at her. He must have walked in from one of the open doors. Mili screamed and ran into another room, not daring to look back. She hid inside the bathroom, only to find another set of eyes staring at her. This time it was a lizard that had dared to come out of its hiding, knowing that the humans were on their way out.

Mili screamed and ran out of the bathroom, only to find another set of eyes. But these eyes were full of warmth and were searching for Mili. It was Kiva. Mili had told Kiva every single time they met since the news of the posting that she would be leaving soon.

Kiva seemed excited with the empty house, the pile of boxes, and large trunks.

"Will you be going to the new place in the truck?" asked Kiva.

"No, of course not." They both giggled as the sound echoed.

"I think we will be going in a plane," Mili added.

"You know, I am leaving before you," informed Kiva.

"Are you coming to the new place too?" asked Mili. They both giggled as Mili's excited voice echoed in the room again.

"No, I am going to my nani's place. She is not well. We are leaving in the evening."

"Oh, okay," said Mili, disappointed. This time there was no echo.

Kiva handed over the piece of paper that was in her hand. "Here, I made a card for you, so that you never ever forget me."

While Mili was opening the card, a warm kiss landed on her cheek. Instantly, Kiva hugged Mili, and Mili hugged her back. They had never really done anything like that before.

Mili's cheeks turned blushing pink. She quickly looked around to see if anyone saw her.

And someone did.

Mili's Mama and Papa and Kiva's Mama and Papa were standing at the door, smiling.

She looked up. She had heard that God was always watching too!

Mili grabbed Gaja's trunk and ran with him into her now empty train compartment. She held Gaja tight and looked at him with the side of her eye.

She wasn't very sure, but she was almost sure, that Gaja was smiling too.

Chapter 6: An Elephant on the Belt

It was almost dinner time when everything was finally done. The truck was loaded and was on its way to the new place, and the house was empty. Now, Mili and her parents were grabbing the last of the things and putting them in their suitcases for the journey the next morning.

"Have you kept the toothpaste and brushes? We will be needing them soon," asked Nikhil.

"Yes. Did you check the backyard?" asked Radha.

"Yes. And where is the lock I had kept aside? We will need it to lock this house. I need to hand over the keys."

"I don't know. Anyway, did you inform the Mess at the guestroom about our dinner? Mili needs to eat soon."

"Haan, haan…" murmured Nikhil, too engrossed in his search.

Mili was also checking the house for any leftover personal belongings. While the house was empty, there were many telltale signs of them having lived there for a year. Some pieces of Mili's old drawings, some broken crayons, Radha's old kurtas torn and turned into dusting cloths, and laces from Nikhil's DMS shoes. Nikhil had explained that they were those big shoes to be worn when soldiers are in combat. Closing up a house was nothing less than a battle.

The cleaning of the house was already arranged for the next day. Just before stepping out of the premises of the house, they took a selfie. Though Mili's legs were not in the frame, they posed beautifully!

The next day, they all reached the airport at seven in the morning. Mili had her honeybee backpack, Radha had her laptop bag and so did Nikhil. Apart from those, there were three other suitcases.

They checked in their bags and went to the security check. The rush was usual, which meant it was maddening! Mili wasn't ready to walk or even hold her bag; it was too heavy. Only Gaja was held tight. Mili was thirsty, and not ready to wait.

The bags went in for scanning, and the 'boys and girls got separated', in Mili's words.

Just when Mili and Radha were about to enter the space enclosed within a curtain for their search, the guard told them to put Gaja in the scanner.

"Noooooo!" screamed Mili as Gaja was put on the conveyor belt. Amongst the sound of the beeping metal detectors, the banging of the plastic trays on the conveyor belt, and the yapping of the passengers, there was one that stood out – Mili's inconsolable crying!

"He will get lost in the machine!" yelled Mili.

She couldn't bear the separation, but nothing could be done. Radha tried to calm her, while also keeping an eye on the bags coming out of the scanner. Far away, Nikhil could hear the cries and tried to frantically gesture that he was coming to them.

"Whose bag is this?" came a question in a loud and stern voice.

It was unmistakenly Mili's honeybee bag.

Nikhil went up to the guard, "It is ours. What happened?"

"There is something in it. Open it."

Stunned, curious and wary at the same time, Nikhil opened it. It was a quick search.

"Oh," he cried, amused and relieved. "So here it is!"

Grinning from cheek to cheek, he held up the missing lock and waved at Radha and Mili.

But they were not looking. Their eyes were fixed on the conveyor belt that was carrying Gaja.

At last, Gaja came out, but upside down. Someone was heard saying, "Look! An elephant on the belt."

Radha grabbed Gaja and handed him to Mili, who finally stopped crying.

Now they were all together – Mili, Gaja, Mili's honeybee bag, Radha and her laptop bag, and Nikhil and his bag.

Mili held Gaja tight. Feeling a little better after the upside-down travel, Gaja could now see things straight and clear. "Distances make the heart grow fonder," he chuckled.

Chapter 7: A Shared New House

A few days had passed since they reached a quiet little town called Garampur in north India. Mili was drawing rain.

Bored of doing nothing in the guestroom, Radha asked, "Mili, do you know how a rainbow is made?"

"Of course. It's very simple to draw, I will teach you."

Radha clarified, "I meant, in the sky how is it formed?"

"It's simple Mama. First, there are two blue clouds," she explained and gestured. "And then a rainbow comes in between," she finished. Satisfied with her answer, she went on with her colouring until the heat caught up with her.

"I am feeling hot," said Mili, fanning herself with her colouring book even though she was sitting right under the fan. Every now and then she would push away the noodle hair off her face with a swift and precise blow from her mouth.

"Get ready to be baked, Mili. Here the summers are too hot, just like an oven, and winters are too cold..."

"Just like a fridge," added Mili.

"Does it snow here?" asked Mili, excitedly.

"No, not really," replied Radha.

Both Radha and Mili were without school. Mili was yet to be admitted to the new school in the middle of the academic year, and Radha had just interviewed at the Army School a day prior.

The only one already deep in work was Nikhil. It was lunchtime, and that's why Mili and Radha were NOT expecting him. There was always too much work to ever come back in time for lunch.

And yet,

"Guess what?" asked Nihil as he stormed into the guestroom. "We've got a house, and it's ready to move in!"

"So soon? That's great!" Radha was excited. She preferred the guestroom stays to be short and sweet.

"Neeeww house? Oh yay!" Mili was excited.

With everything close by in cantonments, it took them two minutes to reach the new house.

"It doesn't look new to me," said Mili as they drove into the driveway.

It was a big old-ish bungalow with a grand front garden and a scarily huge backyard. It had creepers with pink flowers along the garden wall, a raat-rani plant at the gate, a tulsi plant on one side of the garden, a lemon tree, and a dozen mango trees all along the perimeter of the house!

There was no stopping Mili. She ran around in the garden exploring things as if the heat had vanished.

"I'll show you the inside," said Nikhil. Nikhil unlocked the door, and they all stepped in.

"AAAAAHHHH!" That was Mili's first word in this house and the fastest sprint of her life. A beautifully ugly lizard just went scurrying past her.

Well, it was the lizard's fastest crawl, too. The lizard was taken by surprise as it had been a few days since anyone had stayed in the house.

"Not really, it's sealed," replied Nikhil.

"Oh!"

"And here's another room... and ants!" screamed Mili and ran right into Nikhil's arms.

Mili & Gaja Go on a Posting

A wide stream of ants was seen to be migrating from someplace to, well, someplace.

"Relax, Mili. They will go away. Let them do their thing, and let's do ours."

"Yes, let them do their thing, and let us do ours" added Gaja. He didn't like ants one bit.

As they discussed which room would be used for which purpose, Mili found a cute little cupboard and declared, "This will be mine!"

"Wait Mili!" screamed Radha, but it was too late. Mili had opened the cupboard, only to disturb the privacy of a tiny scorpion!

"AAAH!" screamed Mili, running to Radha this time.

"What's that?" Mili asked as drops of sweat rolled down her face.

"It's a scorpion. It's okay. We will see what to do with it later."

"You know, in our training, we would catch such scorpions!" boasted Nikhil.

"Can you catch this one?" asked Mili in awe.

"No, I prefer not," replied Nikhil, walking away.

"Why are they all in our house?" asked Mili, not amused with the zoo-like feel of the house.

"Well, they might ask you the same," replied Radha.

"I hate them!" declared Mili, blowing the noodle hair off her face.

"Shhh, don't say that. They will hear you," said Radha.

"I hate them," repeated Mili, but this time in a whisper.

"Sharing is caring, wasn't that the saying?" asked Gaja in a whisper.

Chapter 8: A Sweet Treat, But for Whom?

"Make it tight!" demanded Mili. Wearing school shoes was never a quick job. It had to be tightened and tightened some more before she could be satisfied. Her noodle hair was neatly tucked in, and Gaja was tucked in her arms.

All three of them were heading to the Army School; Radha as a teacher and Mili as a student. Nikhil was dropping them off.

"It's going to be fun; you will love the school," said Radha, trying to create excitement for the first day. But by then, Mili had started crying inconsolably, holding Gaja tight. "I don't want to go. I want to stay home with you, Papa, and Gaja."

"But Mili, no one is going to be at home. Papa will be at the office, and I will be in your school teaching other children."

"Gaja will be at home!" justified Mili.

"But it's so boring at home, Millilitre. You will learn and enjoy so much in school," said Radha, trying to sound calm.

"And Gaja?" asked Mili.

Hesitating and feeling ridiculous about what she was to say next, Radha replied, "Ammmm. Gaja will be taking a nap. He will not be free to play with you."

They arrived at school. They managed to keep Gaja in the car and take Mili to the classroom. The class teacher, Kavita Ma'am, was preparing for the day ahead. She stopped everything and took charge of the situation. The greetings were overpowered by the sound of crying and the tug-of-war. Mili clung to Radha, while Kavita Ma'am tried to take her. Her touch was soothing, but the situation itself was tough.

Finally, she could get hold of Mili. Holding Mili in her arms, somehow, she assured the worried parents, "I will take care of her. Don't worry. You can go."

They both left, not daring to look back, fearing they would rush and hug Mili.

Radha now reported to the principal and started her yet another teaching tenure. Nikhil left for office.

Days went by, and Mili settled better in the class, but not completely though.

One afternoon, Mili was seen rummaging through Radha's purse.

"What do you want Mili?" asked Radha.

"I am looking for toffees. Was it anyone's birthday today?"

A little irritated, Radha replied, "It was no one's birthday. Haven't I told you not to mess with my...Oh... hmm!" An idea struck her.

The next morning, Radha kept a bar of chocolate in the front pocket of Mili's school bag.

"Mili, give this to ma'am when you reach school," instructed Radha.

"But it's not my birthday... is it?" inquired Mili.

"It isn't. But a kind gesture needs no occasion."

"No, I don't want to give it."

"Why? Don't you like her?"

"I do."

"Then you will take it, it's decided. It's like a 'thank you' for the way she takes care of you in school."

That afternoon, when Nikhil picked them up from school, Nikhil asked her, "Did you give the chocolate to ma'am?"

"Yes," replied Mili from the back of the car.

"What did she say?" asked Nikhil, curious about how it went.

"She took it." There was nothing more to be said.

The next day, when Mili came back from school, she was irritated and complained, "Something was biting me, mama."

"Oh. This place is known for mosquitoes. Tomorrow, I will apply some mosquito repellent."

The next day when Mili came back from school, she complained even more and was irritated even more.

"Hmm, let's try the repellent again tomorrow."

The next day, Mili wasn't irritated—she was angry. "I can't do this anymore. They are troubling me too much." She picked Gaja, sat down, and blew the noodles off her face. Pushing the noodles off her face always helped her make a point!

Radha bent to observe the spots on Mili's knees, and some on her shoulder. "Hmmm... hmmm. Let's check your bag if something rough is rubbing against your skin."

Radha picked up the bag and saw some movement. She got the bag closer, squinted her eyes, and ...screamed, "Ants!"

That was enough to get the mother into supreme action. Radha started taking everything out of the bag, but she stopped the moment she found the culprit—a bar of melted chocolate and a bunch of ants feasting on it.

The bag had a tough time thereon:

It was dropped on the floor.

It was ruthlessly brushed, beaten, and thrashed.

It was washed in the washing machine.

Finally, it was dried in the scorching heat, ready for the next day as if nothing had happened.

Radha and Nikhil didn't say anything to Mili because they didn't want to embarrass her.

Mili didn't say anything because she really had nothing to say about it. She didn't want the chocolate in the first place.

Gaja, too, didn't say anything until he remembered and reminded Mili that the shapeless bar of chocolate was still on the table. Gaja didn't like ants one bit!

Chapter 9: A New Neighbour

One Sunday morning, Mili was woken up by the sound of screams. There was no one in the bed, so she slowly walked around the house looking for everyone. She wasn't expecting what she saw.

There was a boy in her house, maybe 7 or 8 years old. He seemed a little restless and a little rough, and Radha was trying to soothe him. He didn't seem interested in listening to her. As he got uncomfortable, he screamed. Meanwhile, Nikhil made the quickest phone call.

Mili picked one of her stuffed toys, a rabbit, and waved at him. She was used to offering her toys to kids to distract them. But only she knew (and her Mama and Papa) that the toys she offered were never her favourite ones.

The boy almost didn't look at the rabbit and started walking towards something else... or someone else. It was Gaja!

"No!" screamed Mili and rushed to pick up Gaja. But Gaja was what he wanted. The boy tried to pull Gaja away. He seemed to love animals as much as Mili.

They both tugged at Gaja. The only difference was that the boy was looking at Gaja, and Mili was looking at the boy, completely confused as to why he was snatching away Gaja.

"Aarav… Aarav. Mama is here. Relax. See Boo-Boo is also here." Aarav's mother rushed in with a worn-out toy dog.

Radha, too, added, "Your mama is here. It's okay."

Mili was in shock and burst into tears.

Aarav covered his ears and started shaking his head.

Aarav's mother pulled him away and took him to another room.

Things calmed instantly as she handed the dog to him. He looked at the dog, but he never looked up to see his mother!

In a few minutes, Aarav's father rushed to their house in his uniform. He was in the office when Nikhil had called him.

"Come, Mili, let's set you up for some colouring," said Radha taking Mili inside.

"But Mama, who is he? And why was he taking Gaja? Gaja is mine!" affirmed Mili.

"I know, Mili; we will talk about it later."

While Mili was inside colouring, the parents were talking to each other. Aarav was now calm and sitting with his mother, holding the dog tightly in his arms.

While Mili was colouring in another room, she could hear bits of the conversation.

"It has happened a few times... we are so sorry to bother you," the parents were heard saying.

"No no..."

"It's okay..."

"...autistic...so we have to keep an eye on him."

"I came out of the bathroom.... looked for him everywhere."

"Don't worry..."

Once they all left, three of them sat for breakfast. The Poha had become cold by now, just how Mili liked it. Mili neatly kept aside the peanuts on one side of her plate. "Whoo waaas he momma?" asked Mili with Poha stuffed in her mouth.

They are our neighbours, Maj Sharma and his wife Shruti. And the boy's name is Aarav.

"But Papa, why was he pulling Gaja?" asked Mili, grabbing Gaja close to her.

"He is autistic, you can say he is a little different from you."

"He looked fine to me...what was different?"

"Did he look at you?"

"Of course!" Mili replied confidently.

"Think again," Nikhil told Mili.

"Am... no, I don't know," replied Mili, not so confident anymore.

"He did not look you in the eye," added Radha.

"Or anyone else for that matter," added Nikhil.

Radha explained, "Do you like to play with many friends?"

"Yes. I do!"

"Well, autistic children don't. They may have one or two close friends, or they may have none."

"Oh…" said Mili, processing what she was being told.

"Remember that doll you had that could sing rhymes?"

"Yeah, it was my favourite. Where is it? I want it."

"Yes, we will look for it. But that's the kind of toy he may not like to play with. It could disturb him."

"Oh," Mili was still processing. "Where are my peanuts?" squeaked Mili suddenly.

"I ate them, I thought you didn't want them!" replied Nikhil in a petrified tone.

"They are my favourite. I was saving them for the last!" Mili burst into tears and murmured "First Gaja… and now peanuts…"

Radha quickly collected the peanuts from her plate and gave them to Mili.

After finishing them, Mili said, "I'm done. Can I go and play?"

She pushed aside her plate and rushed inside without waiting for an answer.

Inside, she was busy picking up all her soft toys, looking deep into their eyes. And when it was finally Gaja's turn, she picked him up and got him close to her face, looking at his chocolate brown eye.

Just then, that only eye fell on the floor. The tussle was rough on Mili, and on Gaja too.

Chapter 10: The Housewarming Party

Splash!

"I have an idea. We can take one eye out of the bear and put it on Gaja."

Splash!

"That would be unfair... on the bear. See how that rhymes," chucked Radha.

Mili was taking a bath. The best ideas and groundbreaking questions always came to her during bath time. Today's discussion was about how to get some eyes back on Gaja.

"We can make it with *atta* (wheat dough)!"

"It will rot."

Splash!

"We can use stones."

"Too heavy. They won't stay."

Splash!

"Aha, I know, seeds!"

Then we will have rats feeding on the eyes.

"Then, what is your idea?" asked Mili giving up. The wet noodles just wouldn't budge, no matter how hard she blew at them.

"We can prepare eyes with paper or cloth, colour them, and then I'll either stick them or stitch them," replied Radha.

Splash!

It was sorted.

The house had been busy since morning, as there was going to be a housewarming party. Mili had been told that there were going to be lots of uncles and aunties and their children. She walked around, reminding herself to wish them when they came. Apparently, greeting them was the ultimate form of being 'well-behaved'.

Everything was being cleaned, especially the bathrooms. And shelves and surfaces too. Dust always found its way and settled in such places.

Radha was also busy sweeping behind the cupboards and under the tables, removing seeds fallen from Mili's play. Seeds were her favourite ingredients in pretend cooking.

"I'm putting these toys inside, Mili. You don't play with them, and they are making the place look messy."

It was true that some animals really made her yawn when she looked at them. And so, she never played with them. But today was not the day to hide them all, today was the day to show them to whoever was coming.

"No!" said Mili firmly. After much negotiation, it was agreed that they would all be lined up on the bed in the guest bedroom.

Nikhil was in office. He was to pitch in only later in the day. Saturdays were working days too.

"What's on the menu, Mama?"

"Hmm, let's see. There will be hara bhara kebab and some chicken lollipops for snacks. Also, your favourite rajma."

"What's for sweet?"

"Kheer."

"Yum!"

Around lunchtime, Nikhil was back. He was busy ensuring the living room was clean and correctly lit.

Towards the evening, Radha was busy plucking flowers and leaves from the garden to decorate the main areas of the house. Mili followed with Gaja. She was on a mission to find something to use as Gaja's eyes.

"Stones... no, too heavy."

"Seeds... no."

"Leaves... no."

"Mili, come in. Time to get ready!" called out Radha.

Mili dropped everything and rushed in for her favourite thing: getting ready! Radha got her ready in a beautiful yellow cotton frock with balloons embroidered on it.

Around eight in the evening, the house was beautifully lit. There were lights in the garden and the subtle warm light was falling on the beautiful hibiscus flowers. The guests started coming in. Someone was a Captain, somebody a Major, some came alone, while some were with their families.

As Mili took some of the kids inside to her room to play, she remembered to keep Gaja safe from everyone. But where was he?

"Mama, where is Gaja?" Mili asked Radha, who was busy arranging snacks.

"I'm not sure, Mili. Forget about him, and play with your new friends," Radha replied.

Mili returned in ten minutes, this time tugging on Nikhil's shirt. "Papa, where is Gaja?" she asked.

"We will look for him... after some time," replied Nikhil. He was standing with a few guests and made no attempt to move.

Mili returned crying after another ten minutes. This time she had everyone's attention.

"Gaja is missing," said Mili in a barely understandable language.

A lot of guests gave their responses at the same time.

"Oh, poor baby."

"Who is Gaja?"

"Raja is missing?"

"What happened sweetheart?"

"Beta, ro mat. Hum dhoondenge." (*Don't cry, child. We will look for him.*)

"We will help you!"

Everyone found the situation quite adorable, except Radha and Nikhil who found it unnecessary and Mili, who found it extremely painful.

Barring a few, everyone else got up to help Mili. There were five aunties, four uncles, three kids, two parents, and, of course, Mili herself, trying to look for Gaja.

As they went from one room to another, drops of sweat started rolling down their faces.

Mili frantically ran around looking for Gaja, oblivious to the irritated expressions on Radha and Nikhil's faces, and the amused expressions on all others!

There was a weird blend of the aroma of perfumes, sweat, and something else all over the house.

Radha murmured, "What's that smell?"

"Rajma!"

She rushed to the kitchen where she had kept rajma for simmering, hoping to enhance the flavour. The flavour was indeed different now, with notes of caramelization!

One boy declared, "I found him!"

Mili ran to him. "That's not him!" she squeaked.

The other kids got busy explaining to him that what he was holding was not an elephant, but a bear.

The guests, though looking for things, were also busy seeing the house.

One of them joked, "Are you sure Gaja hasn't gone for a walk?"

That's when it struck Mili where Gaja could be. She ran out to the garden. The garden lights were on, and some decorative candles were also laid out. She reached THE spot. She saw Gaja on the grass, but she also saw a set of pitch-black eyes looking at her. Was it Gaja? Gaja had brown eyes, and not to forget, he was now without both eyes!

Then, it moved. It turned out to be a black dog. Mili screamed, grabbed Gaja and started running towards the house. Excited, the dog ran after her, spilling over some candles. One candle fell on a piece of rag, which started to spark.

By then, Mili had reached the door and heard one uncle calling out, "Bruno. Relax. It's okay."

Mili was confused, she wasn't Bruno. She was Mili.

Then the uncle went up to the dog who had caught up with them by now. He put a leash on him. "Sorry

Mili. Since nobody was outside, I took out his leash. But he is very friendly," the uncle grinned.

Nikhil quickly picked up Mili and helped her calm down. Simultaneously, he killed the small fire with his shoes. Radha joined in, not very happy about the Rajma or the chaos. Everyone else went back to their places in the drawing room, warm and sweaty.

Gaja was back in Mili's arms. Gaja didn't have eyes, he smelled of grass, and he had muddy patches all over him. Mili gave him a good shake to check if he was fine. She kept shaking him until Gaja confirmed he was fine, though a little dizzy.

With the sweat rolling down everyone's face, the housewarming was on the mark!

Mili & Gaja Go on a Posting

----------------------------------x----------------------------------

Play with Mili!

Activity 1

Search with Mili – Can you find Mili's favourite food items from the maze of words?

Imli, Kulfi, Kheer, Bhakarwadi, Rajma, Kebab, Poha

Y	I	K	R	X	T	P	I	R	W
D	F	E	L	A	O	Y	E	J	B
W	L	B	V	H	J	E	V	Z	O
A	U	A	A	X	H	M	O	I	B
I	K	B	E	K	C	E	A	H	F
I	L	B	K	P	Y	M	I	X	Q
L	I	M	J	U	X	H	Q	U	R
N	B	B	I	U	I	X	D	N	L
B	A	K	A	R	W	A	D	I	M
L	R	O	G	S	Q	Z	O	H	L

Activity 2
One Word Out

Help Mili find the odd one out from each row and circle it.

1	Army	Flower	Boots	Uniform
2	Truck	Trunk	Posting	Garden
3	Party	School	Decoration	Lights
4	Rajma	Chocolate	Kulfi	Kheer
5	Lizard	Scorpion	Gaja	Ants

Activity 3

Make Many from One

Miscellaneous is one of the longest words in the story. Can you make more words using the same set of alphabets? One word is already made for you.

M I S C E L L A N E O U S

- CELL
- _____
- _____
- _____
- _____
- _____

Activity 4

5 Qualities of Mili

Can you think of 5 words that describe Mili? Write each word inside a petal.

Activity 5
Make Your Mind Map!

Say, it's your birthday and you have to plan a birthday party. Make a mind map to organize all those crazy thoughts – what the menu will include, who will be coming, what games you will be organizing, and so on. Go ahead, make your mind map!

Activity 6
Give the Book Another Name

Did you like the name of the book, 'Mili & Gaja Go on a Posting'? Can you think of another name for the story?

Write it down here _____

About the Authors

Anisha Kotibhaskar

Anisha Kotibhaskar is an artist, a content writer, a trained teacher, a mother, and the author and illustrator of the books titled 'Catch of Day & Other Sibling Stories' and 'A Picnic on a Cloud'. She has two Bachelor's degrees, one in Science, and the other in Education, and a Master's degree in Communication Studies. She was born into an army family and is now married to an army officer. Packing and shifting is what she has always been doing, and that's where her inspiration lies. Anisha aspires to write for children in a way that is delightful and comforting for them.

Sunanda Roy

Dr. Sunanda Roy is an Associate Professor at Adarsha Comprehensive College of Education and Research. She holds a Master's degree in both Educational Psychology and Education, along with a PhD in Education. Teaching students from nursery through secondary school highlights the wealth of her experience with children. Since 2006, she has dedicated herself to the role of Teacher Educator. In 2023, she authored the book "Inclusive Education in Classroom Teaching." She has travelled across India as a child since her father was in a transferable job. This book resonates with her childhood, as it probably will with many readers from similar backgrounds.

www.ingramcontent.com/pod-product-compliance
Lightning Source LLC
LaVergne TN
LVHW021230080526
838199LV00089B/5986